alth

# Lucky Wish Mouse
## White Christmas

## Clara Vulliamy

ORCHARD BOOKS

This is Lucky Wish Mouse.

These are the ten Tinies.

It's Christmas Eve, and there's still lots to do.

Nearly home!

They put up the tree.
It looks a bit bare.
Maybe they can buy some decorations?
But there's nothing in the money box
except for an old sweetie wrapper.

"We'll think of something,"
says Lucky Wish Mouse.

Meanwhile . . .

. . . the ten Tinies are getting on with
the Christmas baking.

101
sweet
treats

Sugar

mmm, these biscuits look delicious...
better try one or two
just to make sure...

Of course, they are all excellent cooks –
they are especially good at
licking the bowl . . .

but slightly less good
at clearing up afterwards.

There's just time for the Tinies
to add a few things to
their Christmas lists . . .

leave out a special snack for
Father Christmas . . .

and finish their mugs of cocoa –

but definitely **no** time for throwing more snowballs . . .

. . . before they hang up
their stockings and
get into bed.

And wait.

And wait.

The stockings are still very,
very
**empty.**

They try and **try** to get to sleep.

"I actually don't think our presents are coming,"
says the biggest Tiny.
"We have to fetch them!
We have to find Christmas!"

"You go!" says each Tiny, in turn,
to the Tiny next to them.

Until there's only the tiniest Tiny left,
at the end of the row.
So she gets out of bed . . .

. . . and slips outside,
out into the night.

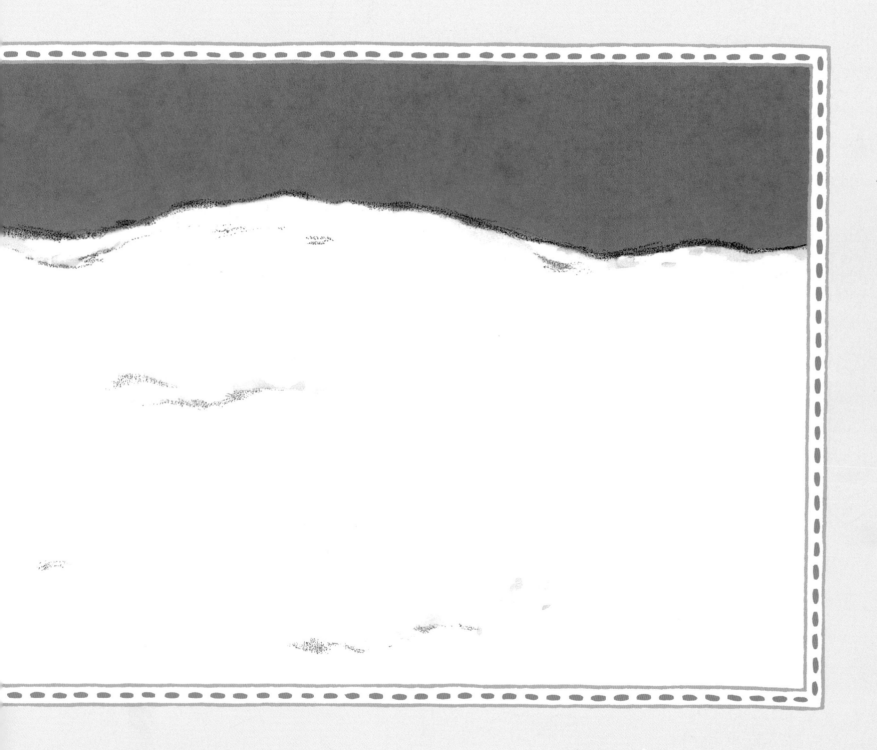

Around
the
corner
she hurries,
with sparkles
in her whiskers,
pink ears and frosty toes . . .

"Is this the way to
the presents?"
she says.

"Is this the North Pole?"

On and on she searches,
Further and further
from home . . .

"I wish Christmas was nearer," she says. "Perhaps it's along here?"

But then
she slips and slides,

landing

**– whoomph! –**

nose-first in snow.

The tiniest Tiny is safe,
but,

"I didn't find Christmas.
I haven't got presents.
I haven't got anything,"
she says.

"But you have!"
says Lucky Wish Mouse.
"Look!"

"Magic snowflakes for our tree!
They collected all around you,
because you are so brave."

Nine Tinies
at the window,
feeling bad . . .

but –

hooray! –

the tiniest Tiny
is **home!**

Lucky Wish Mouse
decorates the tree with
the ten everlasting snowflakes,
sparkling and twinkling . . .

and ten sleepy Tinies are
tucked up together in their cosy, warm bed.

It doesn't really matter
if our stockings are empty,
the Tinies all agree,

as long as we have each other.

ORCHARD BOOKS
338 Euston Road, London NW1 3BH
*Orchard Books Australia*
Level 17/207 Kent Street, Sydney, NSW 2000

First published in 2008 by Orchard Books
This paperback edition published in 2010

Text and illustrations © Clara Vulliamy 2009

A CIP catalogue record for this book
is available from the British Library.

ISBN 978 1 40830 852 3

2 4 6 8 10 9 7 5 3 1
Printed in China

Orchard Books is a division
of Hachette Children's Books,
an Hachette UK company.
www.hachette.co.uk